Tim McGraw's

My Little GiRL

To
_____

From
_____

Date

My Little GiRL

Published in Nashville, Tennessee, by Thomas Nelson. Thomas Nelson is a trademark of Thomas Nelson, Inc.

Thomas Nelson, Inc., titles may be purchased in bulk for educational, business, fund-raising, or sales promotional use. For information, please e-mail SpecialMarkets@ThomasNelson.com.

Cover and interior design by Koechel Peterson & Associates, Minneapolis, MN.

ISBN-13: 978-1-4003-1321-1

Library of Congress Cataloging-in-Publication Data
McGraw, Tim.
  My little girl / Tim McGraw & Tom Douglas ; illustrated by Julia Denos.
     p. cm.
  "Tim McGraw's My little girl."
  Summary: A father and his young daughter share love and laughter as they spend time together and turn an ordinary day into a wonderful adventure.
  ISBN 978-1-4003-1321-1 (hardback)
  [1. Fathers and daughters—Fiction. 2. Country life—Fiction.] I. Douglas, Tom, 1953– II. Denos, Julia, ill.
III. Title.
  PZ7.M478538My 2008
  [E]—dc22
                              2008023073

Printed in the United States of America

08 09 10 11 12 RRD 5 4 3 2 1

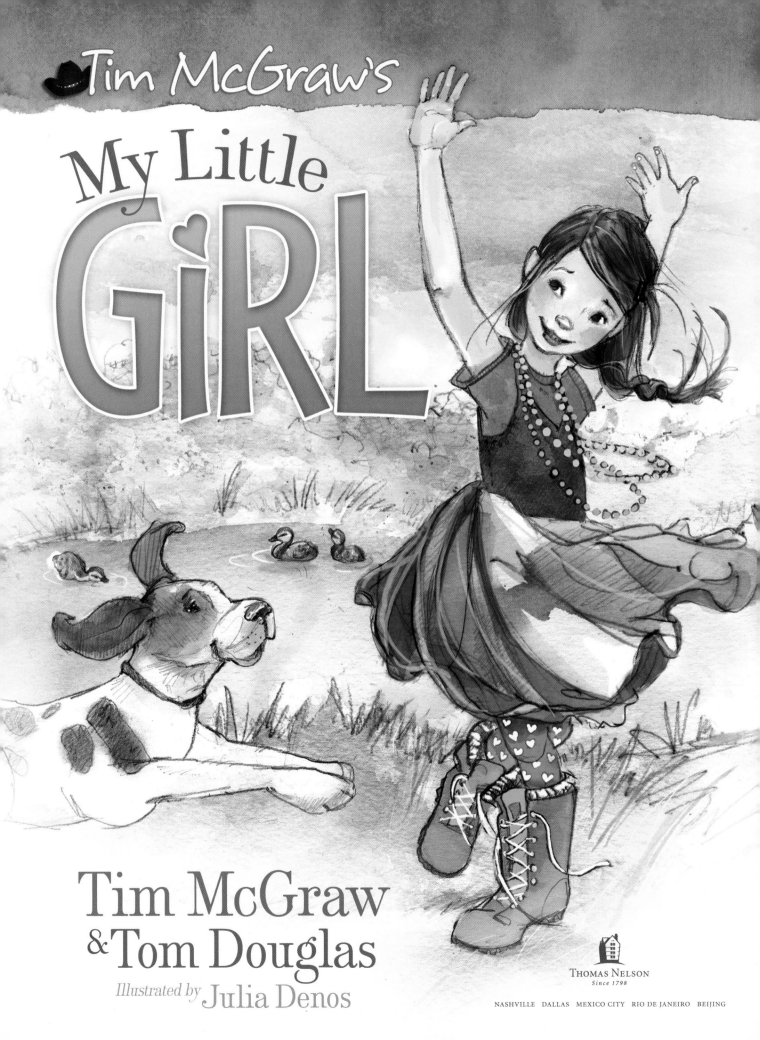

Tim McGraw's
My Little
GIRL

Tim McGraw
& Tom Douglas
Illustrated by Julia Denos

THOMAS NELSON
Since 1798

NASHVILLE DALLAS MEXICO CITY RIO DE JANEIRO BEIJING

This book is devoted to all my girls—
Maggie, Gracie, Audrey, and Faith.
May your dreams come true.
Tim McGraw

"Behold, children are a gift of the Lord. . . ."
Thank You, Lord, for my three gifts.
Tom Douglas

For my Daddy.
Julia Denos

One of my favorite memories of our family is an evening not long ago when Tim and our girls were snuggled up in bed reading a book. Baths were taken, hair was washed and combed, teeth were brushed, and pj's were on . . . all was right with the world.

I was so happy when Tim told me that he and Tom Douglas were asked to write this book, because I believe that books provide a gateway into a child's imagination. They inspire and instill not only knowledge, but also endless possibility. Someone once said that if a child has a story in her heart, she will never be lonely. I'd like to think that is true.

I hope this story provides quality time for fathers and daughters to enjoy each other's company and make memories reading together.

Faith Hill

A "better than chocolate ice cream with sprinkles" kind of day!

Daddy said tomorrow they would have a *spectacular* day—just the two of them. He must be planning something remarkable.

Something unbelievable! Katie couldn't wait.

Palio, her playful spotted puppy who never, ever, ever left her side, thought an ice cream kind of day sounded great.

"This is the start of a day to remember, Palio,"
announced Katie.

"Hmm, what am I going to wear?
If we go to the ball, I must wear my tiara.
But if we go to Africa, I will need
my jungle boots!"

Katie finally decided
to put on...

everything!

"Mornin', Katie girl,"

Dad called from the bottom of the stairs.

"Ready for our big day?

Even though we're doing nothing in particular,

just being together will be spectacular!"

Wait just a time-out minute! Katie thought.

Did he say we were doing—

nothing
in particular?

"First stop, the co-op!" said Dad.

"The co-op? Aw, Daddy, there's nothing spectacular about a co-op.

It's just a bunch of feed and hay

and boring stuff," Katie pouted.

"But there's something new at the co-op,

and I know you'll love it," said Dad.

"Let's go see."

"Bunnies! And baby chicks!" squealed Katie.

"Don't eat my sleeve, little bunny!"

"They sure are cute, aren't they?" said Dad.

"C'mon, Katie. There's something else
I'd like to show you."

"Mommy duck sure is proud of her babies," Dad said.
"But not as proud as I am of my little girl!"

"Those baby ducks look like they are doing a
samba dance all in line," Katie said,
swaying with the rhythm of the duck samba.

"My little girl is the best dancer ever—
just look at you twirl!"

Katie danced and twirled until
she was too dizzy to stand.

Katie plopped down in the grass and leaned back
to look at cloud shapes.

"Look! That cloud looks just like Palio!"

She pointed to the sky.

"And there's a frog about to jump on his head! Do you see it?"

"I think so." Dad grinned.

"Now can you guess what I see?"

"That giant ice cream cone? Or that big, round pickle and strawberry pizza?" Katie guessed as her tummy let out a growl.

"I see a beautiful princess who needs some lunch," Dad said.

"Hey, Daddy, let's spell words with our letters.

We'll see which one of us does better."

Katie spelled L-O-V-E,
but the U dropped to the floor.

Without missing a beat, Daddy
found a U in his soup
and spelled L-O-V-E U M-O-R-E!

"Daddy, swing me all the way
over the sun!" Katie urged.

"Okay, hold on tight, Katie girl."
Dad pushed her high,
and she squealed happily.
"There's one...
two...three!"

"Now it's your turn, Daddy!" Katie announced,
climbing out of the swing. "Hop in."

Katie pushed and pushed with all her might,

but she could only budge Dad a few inches.

They both laughed as he kicked his legs high,
pretending to fly over the setting sun until it disappeared.

"I had a spectacular, nothing-in-particular day,"
Katie declared.

"Better than going to a royal ball?"

Dad teased, as they piggybacked up the stairs.

"What was your favorite part?"

Katie thought for a moment. Then she said,
"Being with you!"

"I'm glad I've got my shades on, 'cause your smile
is as bright as the sun," said Dad.

"Oh, Daddy, everyone knows you don't
wear sunglasses at night," Katie giggled.

"All right, Katie," Dad said.

"Daddy, tell me a story

about when you were

a little boy.

Please?" Katie begged.

"Okay," Dad said. "When I was a little boy,
I used to dream about marrying a very pretty girl."

"Mommy?" Katie guessed.

"That's right!" Dad said. "And I dreamed that we
would someday have a beautiful little girl."

"Me!" Katie laughed.

"...and thank You, God, for Mommy,

and Daddy, and my bestest friend Palio,"

Katie prayed.

Dad hugged and kissed Katie. Then he said,

"I love you, my little girl."

As Katie hugged her daddy tight,

she whispered in his ear,

"Love you more."

"We hope this book inspires Dads and Daughters to spend time together just being Dads and Daughters. Please feel free to write your own story or special 'love you more' moment in the space below."

Tim and Tom